The Wardrobe Monster

To Mum and Dad,
who have listened with eternal good humour to this
and many other stories - Bryony

AN OLD BARN BOOK

First published in 2018 in the UK and Australia and New Zealand
by Old Barn Books Ltd, Warren Barn, West Sussex, RH20 1JW, UK
www.oldbarnbooks.com

Distributed in the UK by Bounce Sales & Marketing
and in Australia and New Zealand by Walker Books Australia

Text and illustrations Copyright © 2018 by Bryony Thomson

The illustrations were created using hand printing & digital techniques

Design by Mike Jolley
Pre-press and Production by Hinotori Media

FIRST EDITION

ISBN 978-1-91064-636-6

10 9 8 7 6 5 4 3 2 1

Printed in Malaysia

MIX
Paper from
responsible sources
FSC® C012700

Paper in this book is certified against the Forest Stewardship
Council® standards. FSC® promotes environmentally
responsible, socially beneficial and economically viable
management of the world's forests.

Bryony Thomson

The Wardrobe Monster

Old Barn Books

Dora had not slept all night and neither had Penguin or Lion or Bear.

It made them grumpy at breakfast...

Grouchy at lunch...

and very groany at going-out time.

But even though she was very, very sleepy,
Dora didn't want to go to bed that night.

She made every excuse
she could think of:

'Lion needs a bath!'

'Bear's still eating.'

'Penguin wants
a story!'

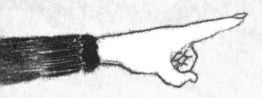

Until Mum got cross; then she had to go.

The problem was the Wardrobe Monster...

'Do you think
it's still there?'
said Lion.

'Tonight will be
different.' said Bear.

Penguin shuddered.

It would start just as
she was drifting off to sleep.

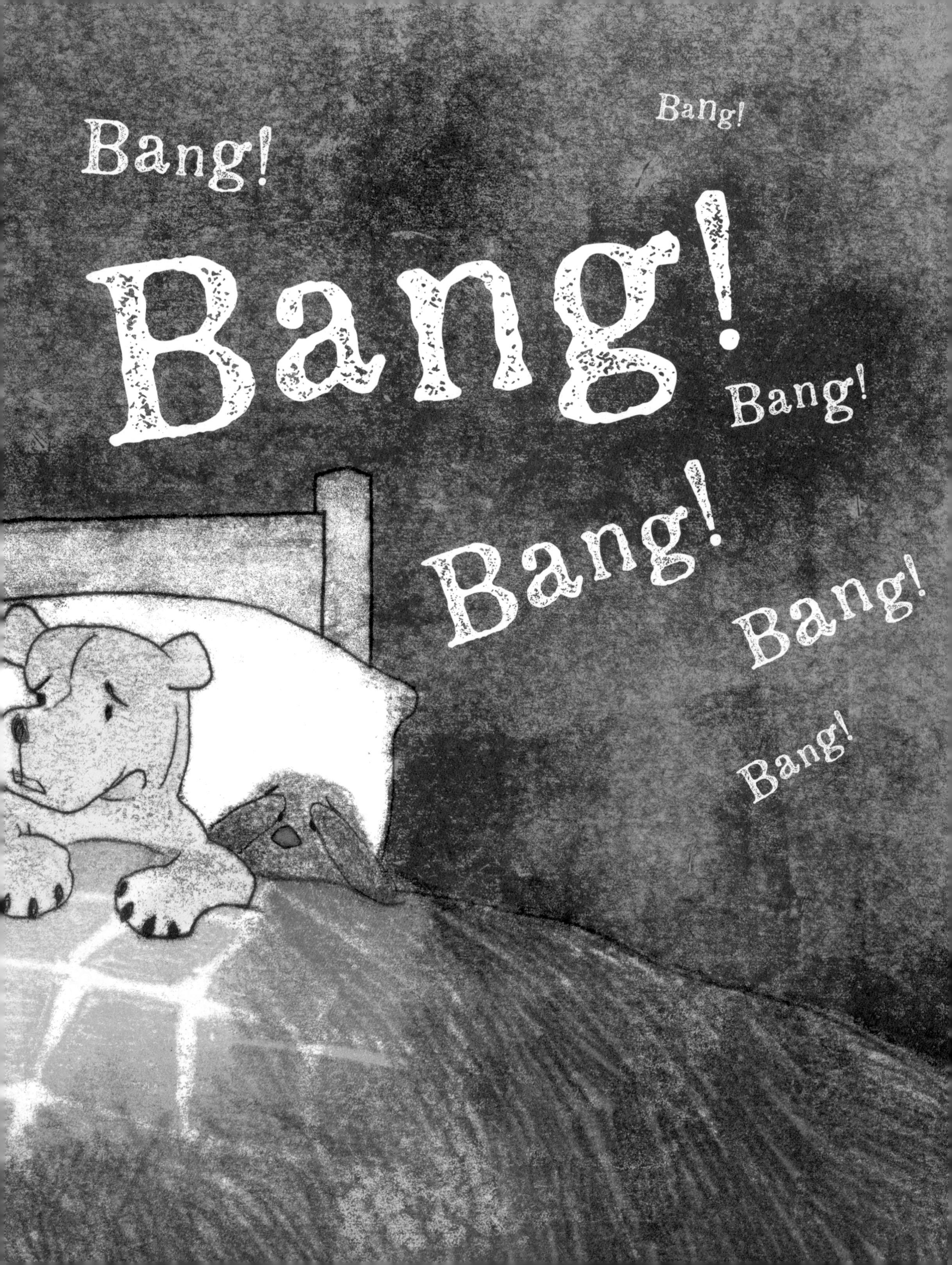
Bang!
Bang!
Bang!
Bang!
Bang!
Bang!
Bang!

Dora and her friends couldn't
agree on what to do.

'You're being silly,' said Bear.
'Wardrobe Monsters aren't real.
Go back to sleep.'
They sounded pretty real though...

'You have to be brave,' said Lion.
'Go and open the wardrobe.'

Bang!

Bang!

Bang!

Penguin pretended to be asleep.
He didn't want to get involved in an argument!

Dora tried to go back to sleep...

Bang!
Bang!

but that really
didn't work.

Bang!

Bang!

So the only
thing to do was
to be brave...

Really, really, **REALLY** brave!

Bang!

Bang!

Bang!

Bang!

Bang! Bang! **Bang!**

Bang! **Bang!**

Dora peered through
the keyhole, but it was
too dark to see.

'**I'm brave,**' she told herself,
'really, REALLY brave.'

'Just a bit further,' said Bear,
'Then I'll have a look.'

'Further,' said Lion,
'Be Brave!'

'Argh!' shouted Lion.

'Oh my!' stammered Bear.
Penguin made a little squeak.

'Help!' whispered Dora. 'Mr Wardrobe Monster, you're squashing us!'
'Oh!' said the Wardrobe Monster, 'I'm terribly sorry!'

'Hello!' said Lion.
'Welcome!' said Bear.
Penguin blinked.

'I was so happy
you opened the door!'
said Wardrobe Monster,
'I heard strange noises outside
my wardrobe and I was
really scared!'

'That was us!' cried Dora,
'We were scared of the noises
coming from INSIDE
the wardrobe.'

'That was me!'
said Wardrobe Monster.

'Why don't you come and sleep with us?' said Dora.
'That way we can all be brave together,' said Lion.
'There's plenty of room,' said Bear.

Penguin frowned.

Finally they were all asleep, until...

'Argh!' yelled Dora.
'What's that?' shouted Wardrobe Monster.
'I'm sure it's nothing,' soothed Bear.
'It must be an Under-the-bed Monster!' roared Lion.

'No...' groaned Penguin, 'It isn't'...

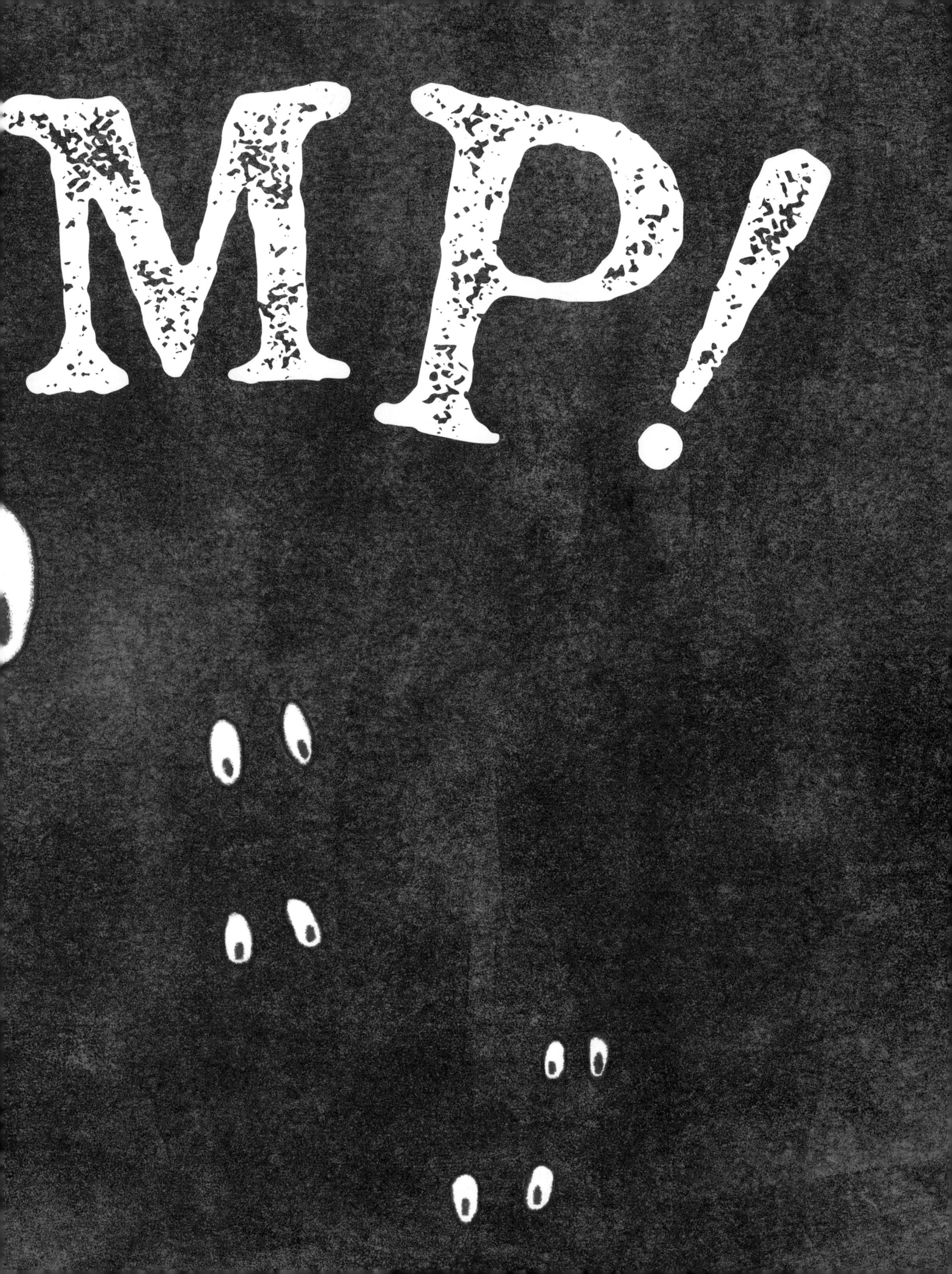
MP!

'It's me. I fell out of bed!'